FOLLOWING MY PAINT BRUSH

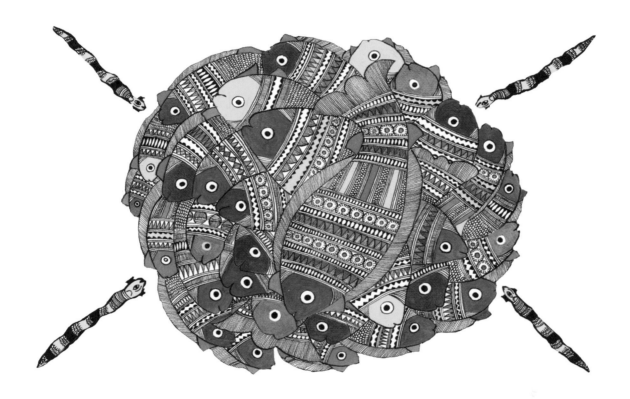

Dulari Devi

Text by Gita Wolf
based on Dulari Devi's oral narrative

I am an artist, but I wasn't always one. This is the story of how it happened.

When I was growing up, I did all kinds of work. My family was poor. I'm the little girl you see in this picture, walking with my mother. We worked in the rice field.

At home, I helped my mother cook and take care of all my brothers and sisters. When we didn't have enough food at home for everyone, our mother was sad.

We went to the market and sold the fish that my father caught. He was a fisherman.

As my mother and I sat with our basket, people would come around, arguing and bargaining for the best price.

To earn more money, we worked in people's houses, washing their dishes.

When we were done, I liked arranging the pots and pans in rows.

Time passed and I grew up, but I still did the same work. I had never gone to school, so I was not trained to do any other job.

Sometimes I wished I could do something else. Everyday was the same, as it had been from the time I was a small girl.

Still, there were some things I enjoyed. I liked children playing. On my way to work, I loved to stop and watch them.

Then one day, when I was passing the village pond, a strange thing happened. As I stood and looked at the children playing, the scene turned into a picture in my mind. It came alive, bright and lively, telling stories. I was happy the whole day, thinking of my picture.

Then another good thing happened.

One day I went to work at a new house as a cleaning woman. It turned out that the woman I worked for was not an ordinary person – she was an artist!

I saw her painting, and I was so delighted that I forgot my own work.

I could think of nothing else. When I reached home, my hands were itching to make something beautiful too. But I had no paper or paints, so I looked around and found some mud near my hut. I took up a handful and began to knead it, smoothing and looking at it from all sides.

And then, slowly, an idea formed in my mind, and I began to turn the mud into something else. It was a bird... I had made a bird!

The next day, when I came to work, my employer was taking a painting class. I was still so excited about my bird that I found the courage to ask her ... could I learn how to paint too? She said ... yes!

What would I draw?

I thought of the fish my mother and I used to sell
in the market, and the strange patterns on them.
I would catch those fish in paint!

It wasn't easy.

First I had to start by learning how to hold a brush in my hand and how to draw a line. Since I had never learned to read and write, this felt very new to me. Then I had to get to know colours.

Once I started, I couldn't stop practising until I got to know the rules of painting.

I've always worked hard.

Once I was confident of how to use my tools, I started to paint subjects that were popular in our village. Here is my painting of Naina Jogin, our local Goddess of the Eye, who keeps away bad luck. It seemed a good place to start.

As time went on I couldn't imagine a single day without painting. It was part of my life.

I couldn't help it, I had to keep working. I found myself wandering around, following my paint brush, turning what I remembered into pictures. I thought of the bad lad in our village, who sat up on a tree smoking.

CHILDREN

THE ICE-CREAM MAN

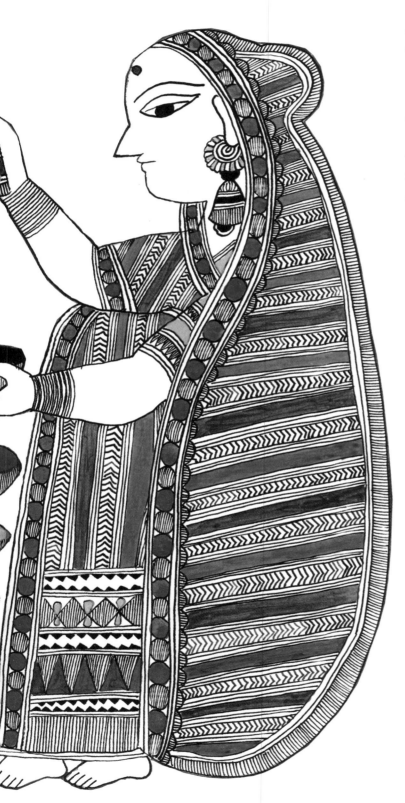

And so I keep painting, and my days are enjoyable.

One day I met some people who made books, and they asked me how I became an artist. My way of telling stories is through painting, so I've painted my story for you here. I was happy doing it, but more than that, I was so proud that people wanted to know about me and what I thought.

And here is my final picture. The woman you see me painting here is myself. I am not just 'a cleaner woman', I am an artist.

I have made a book.